Jane Eyre

THE EXCHANGE

Can you love
someone who
lies to you?

Jane Eyre

BY CHARLOTTE BRONTË
ADAPTED BY JANE E. GERVER

 HAMPTON-BROWN

TO BRIAN—J.E.G.

Hampton-Brown
P.O. Box 223220
Carmel, California 93922
800-333-3510
www.hampton-brown.com

Printed in the United States of America

ISBN-13: 978-0-7362-3137-4
ISBN-10: 0-7362-3137-4

10 11 12 13 14 15 10 9 8 7 6 5 4 3

Contents

Introduction

Jane Eyre takes place in England in the mid-1800s. This was the Victorian Age, a time in English history named after England's Queen Victoria. During the Victorian Age, English society had strict **class** distinctions. People were separated into an upper class, a middle class, and a poor working class.

People in the upper class were rich. They owned land and large homes. They rarely had professions. They hired servants to do their work. The money and the land that the upper class owned passed from parents to the oldest son.

Life was hardest in the lower classes. The servants who were hired to work in the homes of the rich were usually part of the poor lower class. These people worked hard and made little money. They often died young from illness.

The middle class was the largest group. Members of the middle class had some education. They were

Key Concepts

class *n.* rank or status in society

doctors, lawyers, or other professionals. But Victorian women were **excluded** from professional jobs. Women of the poor classes could be servants. They could also work in factories or mills. The most common way for a middle-class woman to achieve success was to marry a rich man. Marriages were not often made for love.

If a middle-class woman *had* to work, few jobs were available. One of these jobs was governess. A governess taught the children of rich families. She taught reading, writing, and music. She even taught correct manners. The governess lived with the family but was considered a paid employee. To be a governess was one way to have work and to have a place to live.

The main character in *Jane Eyre* is a governess for a rich family in Victorian England. She struggles to live her life honestly, even when others do not. She is smart and **independent**, but feels trapped by the strict rules of her class.

At the beginning of the story Jane Eyre is an orphan. She is raised by her middle-class **extended family**.

Key Concepts

exclude *v.* to keep out

independent *adj.* not relying on someone or something else

extended family *n.* family members in addition to parents and children

Their cruelty and **dishonesty** influence her decision to leave their home and become a governess. Jane has to make other important decisions about her life, too. It is hard because she does not know the truth about who she is.

The author of *Jane Eyre*, Charlotte Brontë, had been a governess as a young woman. She used her own experiences to create the character of Jane. Books written by women at this time were rarely published. Brontë wrote under the male pen name Currer Bell. The book became a success. It was then that Brontë revealed she was the author.

FAMOUS PEN NAMES

It is not unusual for writers, even modern ones, to use pen names. Here are some you might recognize, and some that might surprise you.

Real Name	Pen Name	Famous Work
Anne Brontë	Acton Bell	*Agnes Grey*
Mary Ann Evans	George Eliot	*Middlemarch*
Eric Arthur Blair	George Orwell	*Animal Farm*
Samuel Langhorne Clemens	Mark Twain	*Tom Sawyer*
Joanna Rowling	J. K. Rowling	*Harry Potter series*
Chloe Anthony Wofford	Toni Morrison	*Beloved*

Key Concepts

dishonesty *n.* lack of truthfulness

Chapter One

My Story Begins

There was no chance of taking a walk that cold and rainy day. I was glad. My three cousins teased me during the walks. They didn't like me any more than I liked them.

My name is Jane Eyre. My parents had died ten years before, when I was just a baby. Since then, I'd lived with my aunt and her three children at Gateshead Hall.

On this day, my cousins, John, Eliza, and Georgiana, were in the warm **parlor** with their mother. But I was not allowed in.

"Until you can behave like a good girl, you are not to come in here," Aunt Reed told me.

"But what have I done?" I asked.

"Jane, I do not like children who question **their elders**," she snapped.

I **slipped** into a cozy sitting room. There, I sat down

---

parlor formal living room
their elders adults they should respect
slipped went quietly

to read in a window seat. But I was not safe for long.

John flung open the door. He did not see me behind the window curtains. "Lizzy! Georgy!" he called to his sisters. "Jane is not here! Tell Mama!"

Eliza was smarter than her brother. "Jane is in the window seat," she said.

I came out from the curtains **at once**, afraid of being dragged out by John.

"What do you want?" I asked him.

"Say 'What do you want, Master Reed?' " was his answer. "I want to know what you are doing."

John was large and fat for a fourteen-year-old boy. He did not like his mother or sisters. But he liked to **bully** me.

"I was reading." I showed him the book.

"You have no right to take our books," John said. He **snatched the book away**. "You have no money. You should go and beg, not live with rich folks like us. I'll teach you not to touch my books. For they are *mine*—everything in this house will belong to me someday."

He angrily threw the heavy book at me. I fell against

---

at once right away
bully scare
snatched the book away grabbed the book

the door, cutting my head.

"You are a wicked and cruel boy!" I cried. I got up and tried to fight back. I could feel blood **trickling** down my neck from the cut on my head.

Aunt Reed and the servants came rushing in. "Ungrateful girl!" my aunt said. "Lock her up in the red room!"

My aunt's maid, Bessie, took me upstairs to the cold, dark room.

"You have a duty to Mrs. Reed, Miss," Bessie said to me gently. "If not for her, you would **go to the poorhouse**."

This was not news to me. I had heard it many times before.

"Try to be useful and pleasant," Bessie went on. "Otherwise, Mrs. Reed will send you away, I'm sure."

She left me there, sad and lonely. It was the same room where my uncle had died, nine years earlier.

Uncle Reed had been my mother's brother. When my parents died, he **had taken me in**. And when he was dying, he'd made his wife promise to care for me as one of her own children.

....

trickling dripping
go to the poorhouse have no house, food, or clothes
had taken me in took care of me

I cried in the locked room for hours. I'd tried to behave. I'd tried to be good.

But it didn't matter. My aunt did not love me. She only took care of me because she had to.

Left alone, I cried until I fell asleep.

Things got no better as the months went on. I was left out of the holiday parties. And Aunt Reed told my cousins not to spend time with me.

My only friend was a small and ragged doll. And Bessie was sometimes kind. At night she brought me a treat, and she tucked me into bed with a kiss.

One day, I was called into the parlor. A tall man stood there. He stared at me and then turned to my aunt. "She is small. What is her age?"

"Ten years," Aunt Reed replied.

"What is your name, little girl?" the man asked me.

"Jane Eyre, sir," I said.

"Well, Jane, are you a good child?"

Aunt Reed sniffed and shook her head. **"The less said on that, the better."**

"A naughty little girl is a **sad sight**," the man said

"The less said on that, the better." "We should not talk about that."

sad sight terrible thing to see

with a sigh.

"Mr. Brocklehurst, Jane is a liar," Aunt Reed said. "That is her biggest fault. If she goes to Lowood School, you will need to **keep an eye on her**. Train her to be useful and **humble**. And I wish her to spend all vacations there."

Mr. Brocklehurst nodded. "You have made a wise choice in schools, Mrs. Reed. Our pupils are quiet and wear plain clothes. Jane will be taught **her proper place in life**."

He handed me a book of prayers, then left the house. I glared at my aunt.

"I am *not* a liar!" I blurted out. "If I were a liar, I'd say I loved you. But I do not love you! I hate you. I will never call you aunt again!"

My aunt looked frightened. "Children's faults must be corrected," she said.

"Lying is not my fault!" I cried out. "Send me away to school soon—I hate living here!"

"I will indeed," muttered my aunt.

It took only a day or two to pack my few belongings. I left Gateshead Hall on a cold January morning. Bessie

....

keep an eye on her watch her very carefully

humble not proud; modest

her proper place in life how to behave and follow the rules

packed me some biscuits for the long trip.

A coach pulled by four horses and filled with passengers drew up to the gate. I climbed on board—but not before I hugged and kissed Bessie good-bye.

That was how I left Gateshead . . . and **headed for the unknown**.

---

headed for the unknown began a new life

BEFORE YOU MOVE ON...

1. **Summarize** Reread pages 11–13. Why is Jane living at Gateshead Hall?

2. **Comparisons** How does Aunt Reed treat Jane? How does Bessie treat Jane? What are the differences?

LOOK AHEAD Read pages 17–24 to find out if life is better for Jane at Lowood School.

Chapter Two

Lowood School

I remember little of the long journey to Lowood. As night approached, our coach headed into a **wooded valley**. A wild wind whistled around us.

Soothed by the sound, I fell asleep. Suddenly the coach stopped.

"Is there a little girl called Jane Eyre here?" a servant asked. **I was handed down**, and the coach rumbled away.

The servant led me inside a large building. She left me alone in a parlor, warming my hands at a blazing fire.

The school **superintendent**, Miss Temple, soon entered the room. She was tall, with kind brown eyes.

"You must be tired," she said gently to me. "Is this the first time you have left your parents, little girl?"

I explained that I had no parents. She asked me how

---

wooded valley land between hills covered with trees
I was handed down The driver helped me get out of the coach
superintendent director, supervisor

old I was, my name, and if I could read, write, and sew. Then she sent me off to bed in a long dormitory lined with thirty or forty beds.

Surrounded by silence, I fell asleep.

A loud bell woke me. It was still dark, but the girls all around me were getting out of bed and putting on handmade brown **frocks**. I dressed, shivering in the bitter cold.

When the bell rang again, we marched downstairs to the dining room for breakfast. How glad I was! I felt sick from not eating.

The room was huge and gloomy. Bowls of steaming porridge sat on two tables. The food smelled terrible. I saw some of the girls wrinkle their noses.

"Disgusting! The porridge is burned again!" they **murmured**.

"Silence!" shouted a teacher.

After prayers and a **hymn**, the meal began. I was starving and quickly ate a few spoonfuls. But I soon realized how bad the cereal was.

Each girl tasted her food and tried to swallow it. But

Surrounded by silence In the quiet room

frocks dresses

murmured said quietly

hymn song

no one could.

When breakfast was over, we went to the schoolroom for our classes. Eighty girls sat on benches, softly **reciting their lessons**. The older girls were taught geography and music. My class learned history, grammar, writing, and arithmetic.

At noon, the bell rang, and Miss Temple stood up to make an announcement. She smiled. "This morning, you could not eat the breakfast. You must be hungry. You will be served a lunch of bread and cheese."

How good that food tasted! After lunch, each girl put on a straw **bonnet and a cloak**. We went out to the garden for exercise and play.

A fog hung over the damp garden. The stronger girls ran about. But many girls were pale and thin. They stayed on the porch. I heard them coughing often.

"Does this house belong to Miss Temple?" I asked one girl sitting nearby.

"Oh, no!" she said with a sigh. "We wish it did! She reports to Mr. Brocklehurst. He buys all of our food and the material we use to make our clothes."

The bell **called us to an early dinner** of potatoes

....

reciting their lessons reading their lessons aloud

bonnet and a cloak hat and a loose coat

called us to an early dinner rang to let us know it was time to eat the main meal with shreds of **rusty-looking** meat. I wondered if every meal would taste this bad.

More lessons followed. At five o'clock, we were each given half a slice of brown bread. After more studying, water and thin oatcakes were **handed out**. Then we went up to bed.

The next few weeks were hard for me. Our plain dresses and aprons did not protect us from the winter weather. We had no boots, and snow got into our shoes and melted.

And there was not enough food. I was hungry all the time. The bigger girls took food from the smaller ones. Many times I was left with only a **morsel**.

One afternoon, Mr. Brocklehurst arrived in the schoolroom.

"Twice in the past two weeks, a lunch of bread and cheese was served to the girls. That is *not* in the rules! Who did this? And why?" he demanded.

Miss Temple stepped forward. "I did," she confessed. "The breakfast was badly cooked. No one could eat it. I could not let the girls wait until midday dinner."

....

rusty-looking reddish
handed out given to us to eat
morsel small piece; crumb

Mr. Brocklehurst shook his head angrily. "I have a plan in **bringing up** these girls," he said. "They must be patient and strong in spirit! How will they learn such things if they are fed treats?"

He looked around. I held up my chalk slate to hide my face. I remembered what Mrs. Reed had said to him about me. I didn't want him to see me.

All at once, my slate slipped from my hand and crashed to the floor.

"Careless girl!" said Mr. Brocklehurst. "It is the new **pupil**, I see. Come forward!"

He made me stand on a high stool in the middle of the room.

"Children," began Mr. Brocklehurst. "Do not play with this girl. Teachers, watch her carefully. For this child is a liar! She must stand for a half-hour on that stool. No one must speak to her for the rest of the day." Then he left the room.

I almost began to **sob**. Then a student passed by and **gave me a smile of friendship**. I took a deep breath and held my head up high. Mr. Brocklehurst would not win—I would be stronger than anyone!

....

bringing up teaching

pupil student

sob cry

gave me a smile of friendship looked at me kindly

As the months went by, I **grew happier** at school. Miss Temple was kind to me, and I made a few friends.

My classes went well, too. I began to learn French and drawing. When warmer weather came, we took walks among the flowers and trees.

But with the warm weather came sickness. **A fever swept through** Lowood School. Many students, weak from the harsh winter, fell ill. Some even died.

Finally the illness in the school ended. But the townspeople were angry. They checked the school and saw how poorly we were fed and clothed. They discovered how cruel Mr. Brocklehurst had been.

New people were put in charge. Things **improved**, and Lowood became a fine school.

I stayed there for six years as a student. I worked hard and rose to be the top student in the highest class.

After that, the school gave me a job as a teacher. I taught younger girls reading, writing, sewing, drawing, and more.

During my years at Lowood, Miss Temple guided me: first as my teacher, then as my friend. But after I had been there for eight years, she married and moved

---

grew happier became happier

A fever swept through Many students became ill with fever at

improved got better

far away.

I grew tired of Lowood. What was keeping me there now? **I wondered what lay beyond the school's gates.** What kind of life could I make for myself?

I decided to **seek work as a governess**, teaching children in a family. I placed an advertisement in the town's newspaper.

After one long week, I heard from a Mrs. Fairfax at Thornfield Hall. **She offered me a position!**

I told the school that I wished to take the job. But Mrs. Reed had to give me permission. I wrote her a letter.

"You may do as you please," my aunt wrote back curtly.

On my last night at Lowood, I packed my few clothes in a trunk—the same trunk I had arrived with eight years earlier. Just then, I was told that a visitor wished to see me downstairs.

A woman rushed out of the parlor. "You've not forgotten me, Miss Jane?" she said.

"Bessie! Bessie!" I cried happily, hugging her. It was Aunt Reed's maid!

....

I wondered what lay beyond the school's gates. I was curious about how people lived outside of school.

seek work as a governess look for a teaching job

She offered me a position! She gave me the job!

"When you wrote to your aunt, I decided to visit you before you **went off on** your new life," Bessie said.

Then she grew quiet. "There's something I need to tell you, Miss. Seven years ago, a man came to Gateshead. He was looking for you—his last name was Eyre! Mrs. Reed said you were away at school. He could not stay; he was **sailing to a foreign land**. He looked like quite a gentleman. I believe he was your father's brother!"

I **hesitated**. I had an uncle, and he'd come looking for me!

"So he left the house?" I finally asked.

"Yes, and Mrs. Reed was rude to him. She always did say that the Eyres were poor and not to be trusted."

I shook my head sadly. Would my uncle ever come looking for me again?

The next day, I saw Bessie as we waited for our coaches. Bessie's coach took her back to Gateshead.

And mine took me to a new life at Thornfield Hall.

---

went off on started

sailing to a foreign land going to a far away place

hesitated stopped to think

BEFORE YOU MOVE ON...

1. **Cause and Effect** At first, the girls at Lowood are hungry and sick. What causes things to change?

2. **Character** Why does Jane choose to leave Lowood school? What does this show about her personality?

LOOK AHEAD Read pages 25–32 to see if Jane's life at Thornfield is what she expected.

Chapter Three

A Curious Laugh

My journey to Thornfield took more than seventeen hours. The October night was **raw and misty**. I had time to think as the one-horse coach rattled along.

Did Mrs. Fairfax live alone with her little girl? "I hope Mrs. Fairfax will not be like Mrs. Reed," I prayed.

About ten minutes after passing a church, we reached a set of gates in a wall. The driveway led to a large house, with candlelight in only one window.

"Will you walk this way, **ma'am**?" asked a young maid at the front door.

I followed her to a **snug** room. An elderly lady sat knitting by the fire.

"How do you do, my dear?" she said kindly. "I am Mrs. Fairfax. Do sit down. Your luggage will be taken up to your room." She turned to the maid and said, "Leah, please bring us some sandwiches."

....

raw and misty cold and rainy
ma'am lady, madam
snug warm, cozy

She treats me like a visitor, not a governess, I thought, watching as Mrs. Fairfax served the food herself.

"**Shall** I see Miss Fairfax tonight?" I asked politely.

"Miss Fairfax? Oh, you mean Miss Varens, your pupil," Mrs. Fairfax replied.

"She is not your daughter?" I asked, puzzled.

"No, I have no family," Mrs. Fairfax explained. "I am so glad you have come. Thornfield can get quite lonely. We have Leah, and John, who drove you here, and his wife, the cook."

She smiled and added, "Just last month little Adèle Varens came to live here. She makes the house **come alive**. And now you are here, too!"

She then showed me to my room. We walked up a staircase made of dark oak. The long chilly hallway on the second floor looked as if it belonged in a church, not a house.

I was pleased to find my new bedroom small and cozy. I fell asleep quickly and slept **soundly** all night.

The next morning, I walked downstairs and out onto the lawn. The house was **imposing, with battlements**

....

Shall Will

come alive cheerful and busy

soundly well

imposing, with battlements big and threatening, with places for soldiers to guard the house around the top. Loudly cawing crows flew above it.

Mrs. Fairfax appeared at the door. "How do you like Thornfield?" she asked.

I told her I liked it very much.

"It is a pretty place," she agreed. "But it will get out of order unless Mr. Rochester comes to live here permanently—or visits it more often."

"Mr. Rochester!" I exclaimed. "Who is he?"

"The owner of Thornfield," Mrs. Fairfax said. "You did not know that?"

"I thought Thornfield belonged to you," I said.

"To me? What an idea!" she said, laughing. "I am only the housekeeper."

"And the little girl—my pupil?"

"**She is Mr. Rochester's ward.** He asked me to find a governess for her. Ah, here she comes with her nurse, Sophie."

A **delicate** girl of seven or eight came running over. She had curls **falling down** to her waist, and a thin, pale face.

"Is this my governess?" Adèle asked her nurse in

....

She is Mr. Rochester's ward. Mr. Rochester is her guardian.
delicate tiny
falling down that went

French. Her nurse answered "yes" back in French.

"Adèle was born in France," Mrs. Fairfax explained to me. "When she first came here, she could speak no English at all. Now she speaks a little, but mixed with French."

Luckily, I had studied French at Lowood and was able to chat with the girl during breakfast. Adèle told me about the clean, pretty town where she had lived in France.

"My mama is not alive anymore," Adèle said. "She taught me to sing and dance. May I sing for you now?"

After the little performance, I took her to the house's library. This would be our classroom. Mr. Rochester had left us many suitable books, a piano, an easel, and two globes.

I taught Adèle until noon, when I allowed her to return to Sophie. Mrs. Fairfax then showed me around the house. The dining room was beautiful and **stately**. It had a stained-glass window and purple chairs and curtains. The **drawing room** was also lovely, with a flowered carpet and large mirrors.

---

stately elegant; large
drawing room living room

Everything was clean and tidy. "Mr. Rochester's visits are rare," Mrs. Fairfax said. "**But they are always unexpected.** So I keep the rooms ready for him. Would you like to see the rest?"

What a tour I had! The large front bedrooms on the second floor were grand-looking.

Over the years, older beds and chests had been moved up to the third floor. A long, narrow hallway separated the front and back rooms. It was lined with small black doors, all of them shut.

I liked the **hush and gloom** that filled those darkened rooms. Tapestries hung on the heavy oak doors and walls.

"The servants have smaller rooms in the back. No one ever sleeps here," Mrs. Fairfax said. "If there were a ghost at Thornfield, **this would be its haunt**."

"You have no ghost, then?" I asked with a shiver.

"None that I ever heard of," Mrs. Fairfax replied, smiling. "Come, I'll show you the view from the roof."

I followed her up a narrow staircase to the attic. Then we climbed a ladder up through a trapdoor to the roof.

....

But they are always unexpected. We do not know when he will come to visit.

hush and gloom quiet and shadows

this would be its haunt this is the room where it would live

I leaned over the battlements and viewed the grounds spread out below: a **velvet** lawn, a field, dark woods, the country church, and a **ring** of hills.

I could hardly see my way back down the ladder. The attic was so dark after the bright blue sky above.

Mrs. Fairfax stayed behind to fasten the trapdoor. I groped my way down the narrow staircase to the third floor.

Then I heard something, the last sound I expected to hear in such a quiet place. **A curious** laugh!

The ghostly sound stopped, then began again, louder this time. It seemed to echo in every room.

"Mrs. Fairfax!" I called out. "Did you hear that laugh? Who is it?"

"Some of the servants, very likely," she answered. "Perhaps Grace Poole. We use her for sewing and to help Leah with the housework. Grace sews in one of these rooms. Leah and she are often noisy together."

The strange laugh sounded again, low and ending in **an odd murmur**.

"Grace!" called Mrs. Fairfax.

....

velvet smooth
ring circle
A curious An unusual
an odd murmur a strange noise

I did not really expect anyone to answer. But the door nearest me opened, and a servant came out. The woman was solidly built, with red hair and a hard, plain face. She did not look like a ghost at all.

"Too much noise, Grace," said Mrs. Fairfax. "Remember the rules!" Grace curtsied silently and went back into the room. And Mrs. Fairfax and I returned downstairs to light and cheerfulness.

The weeks **became routine**. Adèle was not hard to teach, though she was rather spoiled.

But when I took walks alone, I began to feel **restless**. The servants were all pleasant. Yet I wanted to meet more people, to see more things.

The only thing that calmed me was to walk along the house's third-floor corridor. As I paced, I imagined new experiences and **felt less trapped**.

Very often when on the third floor, I heard Grace Poole's laugh—the same slow "ha! ha!" as the first time. I also heard her murmurs, stranger than her laugh.

And sometimes I saw her. She would come out

---

became routine were all the same
restless bored, uneasy
felt less trapped could think about life outside of the house

of her room with a **basin** or a tray, go down to the kitchen, and then return. I tried to talk with her several times, but she **seemed a person of few words**.

....

basin bowl

seemed a person of few words did not want to talk

BEFORE YOU MOVE ON...

1. **Comparisons** How is the way Mrs. Fairfax treats Jane different from Jane's treatment at Lowood or Gateshead?

2. **Mood** What gives this chapter a mysterious mood?

LOOK AHEAD Read pages 33–42 to find out if Thornfield becomes a more exciting place to live.

Chapter Four

I Meet a Stranger

October, November, and December passed by. In January, I gave Adèle a day off from her lessons and offered to mail a letter for Mrs. Fairfax. The two-mile walk to town would be a pleasant way to spend the afternoon.

I left Adèle with a doll and a book, put on my bonnet and cloak, and **set out**.

The quiet **lane** was surrounded by empty fields. Little brown birds, **nestled in the hedges**, looked like autumn leaves. I walked quickly to get warm.

A mile from Thornfield, I walked up the hill to a fence and sat down. Wrapped in my cloak, I did not feel the cold. A little brook nearby had overflowed a few days before. A sheet of ice covered the road.

From my seat I could look down on Thornfield. It **loomed** large in the valley, with woods behind it. I sat

....

set out went on my way to town
lane road
nestled in the hedges resting in the bushes
loomed looked

until the sun went down, **streaking** the sky with red.

As I watched the moon rise over town, I heard a **clattering** sound. A horse was coming. The road curved, so I was not able to see the animal. I sat still to let it pass.

Just before the horse appeared, I heard another noise. A large black-and-white dog glided by, followed by the horse and its rider. They passed me, and I began my walk again. Then came a sliding sound and a clattering tumble.

I turned and saw that the horse and man had fallen on the ice. The dog came **bounding** back. He barked when he saw his master and the groaning horse.

Who else could help but me? I walked over and asked, "Are you injured, sir? Can I do anything?"

"Stand to one side," answered the traveler. He rose slowly to his feet. He helped the horse to rise, too.

"Down, Pilot!" the man said sternly to the dog. He limped over to the fence, rubbing his foot and leg, and sat down.

"If you are hurt, sir, I can **fetch** someone from either Thornfield Hall or from town," I said.

....

streaking filling, coloring
clattering loud, rattling
bounding jumping, running
fetch go and get

"Thank you, no. I have no broken bones, just a sprain," the man replied. He stood up and **winced**. "Ugh!"

In the daylight still left, I plainly saw him. He was about thirty-five or forty years old and of average height. His face was stern, with a **heavy brow**.

I had no fear of the stranger. If he had been a handsome young gentleman, I would not have dared to ask questions or offer help. If he had smiled and waved me on, I would have left. But his frown somehow **put me at ease**.

"I cannot think of leaving you alone in this lane, sir, at so late an hour, until I see that you can mount your horse."

He glanced at me. "You should be at home yourself," he said. "Do you live in this neighborhood?"

"I live just below and am not afraid when there is moonlight," I answered. "I am going to town to **post** a letter."

"Do you live at that house?" the man asked, pointing to Thornfield Hall.

"Yes, sir."

---

winced trembled, flinched
heavy brow look of sadness
put me at ease made me feel comfortable
post mail

"Whose house is it?"

"Mr. Rochester's," I said.

"Do you know Mr. Rochester?" he asked.

"No, I have never seen him."

"You are not a servant . . ." he **mused**, looking me over.

"I am the governess," I told him.

"Ah, the governess!" he exclaimed. "Well, perhaps you can help me. Come over here, please," he requested. Leaning on my shoulder, he **limped** to the horse and managed to mount it.

"Now **make haste** to town and return home as fast as you can," he instructed me. Then he rode away, the dog close behind him.

I continued on to the post office. My help had been needed, and I was pleased. The man's face was new to me, too, and I liked that.

After mailing the letter, I hurried home. The front hall was dark, but a warm glow came from the open dining room. I **spied** a group, including Adèle, inside. The door closed, and I hurried to Mrs. Fairfax's parlor.

She was not there, but a large dog was—sitting alone

....

mused guessed, figured
limped walked in pain
make haste go quickly
spied quietly looked at

on the rug. He was black-and-white, like the dog in the lane.

"Pilot," I said. The dog shuffled over and wagged his tail. I **rang** for Leah.

"Whose dog is this?" I asked her.

"He came with Mr. Rochester, who just arrived," Leah said. "Mrs. Fairfax and Miss Adèle are with him in the dining room. John has gone to fetch a doctor, for the master has had an accident. His horse fell on some ice in the lane, and his ankle is **sprained**."

"Ah, I see," I said. Now I knew who the mysterious traveler was.

By the following morning, Thornfield had changed—and for the better. The house now had an owner in it. Every hour or so, there was a knock at the door or a ring of the bell. **Footsteps crossed the halls**, and new voices spoke.

We moved the schoolroom upstairs, as Mr. Rochester needed the library for meetings. Adèle was not easy to teach that day. She kept running to look over the banister for him.

....

rang called

sprained hurt

Footsteps crossed the halls We could hear the sound of people walking in the hallways

After the lessons, Mrs. Fairfax said to me, "Mr. Rochester would like you and Adèle to join him for tea this evening. Change your frock—I always dress up for the evening when he is here."

I put on a black silk dress, along with a pearl brooch that Miss Temple had given me at Lowood. Then I nervously went down to the drawing room.

Adèle sat on the floor, with Pilot beside her. Mr. Rochester sat on a couch, his foot on a cushion. I recognized him at once. His mouth, chin, and jaw were grim-looking, almost ugly.

"Let Miss Eyre be seated," Mr. Rochester ordered stiffly.

We sipped our tea in silence. Then Adèle piped up, "**Monsieur** Rochester, I know you have brought me presents. Don't you have one for **Mademoiselle** Eyre?"

"**Are you fond of** presents, Miss Eyre?" Mr. Rochester asked gruffly. He stared at me with dark, piercing eyes.

"I hardly know, sir," I said. "I am not used to them. In any case, I am a stranger to you. I do not deserve a gift."

Monsieur Mister (in French)
Mademoiselle Miss (in French)
Are you fond of Do you like

"Nonsense," scoffed Mr. Rochester. "**Adèle's studies have improved greatly**, thanks to you."

When our tea was finished, Mr. Rochester invited me to sit near him by the fire. He asked me many questions about Lowood and my courses.

Then without warning, he looked at his watch and said abruptly, "Nine o'clock! Take Adèle to bed, Miss Eyre." With a wave of his hand, he added curtly, "I wish you all good night."

After putting Adèle to bed, I joined Mrs. Fairfax in her rooms. "Mr. Rochester seems very moody," I said.

"He may be, but I am used to **his manner**," Mrs. Fairfax said. "Besides, **he has painful thoughts of family troubles**."

"I thought he had no family," I pointed out.

"Not now, but he used to," Mrs. Fairfax said. "His elder brother died nine years ago. Edward Rochester has been master of Thornfield Hall ever since. Yet he spends less than two weeks at a time here. Perhaps he thinks it's gloomy."

I would have liked to know more, but it was clear that Mrs. Fairfax could not—or would not—tell me.

Adèle's studies have improved greatly Adèle is learning very well now

his manner the way he acts

he has painful thoughts of family troubles he thinks about his family and he becomes very sad

I saw little of Mr. Rochester in the next few days. In the mornings he tended to business. In the afternoons men came by and sometimes stayed to dine. When his ankle was better, he rode out to visit people and returned at night.

If we passed in the halls, he merely nodded or glanced at me. Sometimes he gave a bow and a slight smile.

One day, he **sent for me** after dinner. He looked less glum than before and caught me staring at him.

"Do you think me handsome, Miss Eyre?" he asked.

My answer slipped out without warning. "No, sir."

"**You are indeed blunt!**" he said. "I wish to learn more about you. Speak!"

I frowned. "You do not have the right to **command me that way**, sir."

"You are right," he agreed. "I have plenty of faults." He paused, and a brooding look crossed his face. "I **started off on the wrong track** when I was twenty-one."

....

sent for me asked me to come see him
You are indeed blunt! You say what you mean!
command me that way tell me what to do
started off on the wrong track got into trouble

"It seems to me, sir," I began, "that you might try to change. In a few years, you could be happier." I rose and added, "I must put Adèle to bed now."

"Do you never laugh, Miss Eyre?" Mr. Rochester asked. "No doubt Lowood School kept you from being merry. But in time, I think you will be more lively with me. Good night!"

As the weeks passed, I **warmed to** Mr. Rochester. We talked often, though he did most of the talking. He liked telling me about the world, and I liked listening.

He told me about Adèle's mother, a friend of his in France. When she ran away with a musician, Adèle was left with no one to **raise** her. So Mr. Rochester had brought Adèle to England.

Over time, he became more polite when we ran into each other. He always had a word and sometimes a smile for me. This made my time at Thornfield much happier.

However, I could not forget Mr. Rochester's faults.

---

warmed to began to like
raise take care of

He remained overly proud, moody, and rude to others.

But was Mr. Rochester still ugly in my eyes? Not anymore—his face was the one I most liked to see, and he was **cheerier in a room than any fire**.

....

cheerier in a room than any fire more pleasant to be around than a warm fire

BEFORE YOU MOVE ON...

1. **Cause and Effect** Reread page 37. To Jane, what makes Thornfield better?

2. **Evidence and Conclusions** Reread pages 40–42. Mr. Rochester wants to be Jane's friend. List 3 details that support this.

LOOK AHEAD Read pages 43–52 to see who is hiding a terrible secret at Thornfield.

Chapter Five

Fire!

After Mr. Rochester had been at Thornfield for eight weeks, I awoke suddenly late one night. A strange murmur came from above my room.

I sat up in bed. The sound stopped. I tried to sleep again, but my heart beat anxiously. The clock down the hall struck two. Just then, I heard **fumbling** at my door!

"Who's there?" I called. No one answered. I was **chilled with fear**.

Pilot often liked to **lumber** upstairs from the kitchen to Mr. Rochester's doorway at night. The idea calmed me, and I began to **doze**.

Then came a laugh—low and deep—almost at the keyhole of my locked door! I got out of bed, shivering. The laugh came again, followed by a gurgle and a moan.

Before long, I heard footsteps. They went down the

fumbling something moving
chilled with fear so afraid I was shivering
lumber walk slowly
doze sleep

hall, toward the stairs leading to the third floor. The staircase door opened and closed. Then all was still.

Was that Grace Poole? I wondered. It was impossible to stay by myself any longer. I had to find Mrs. Fairfax! I threw on a dress and shawl, unbolted my door, and opened it with a trembling hand.

A lit candle in a holder stood on the carpet. The air in the hallway was dim and smoky. There was a strong smell of something burning!

A partly opened door creaked. It led to Mr. Rochester's bedroom—and smoke was rushing out from it!

I instantly forgot Mrs. Fairfax, Grace Poole, and the evil-sounding laugh. I dashed into Mr. Rochester's room. **Tongues of flame darted around** the bed. The bed curtains were on fire!

Mr. Rochester lay fast asleep in the middle of the blaze. "Wake up! Wake up!" I screamed. I shook him, but he only muttered and turned. The smoke had left him **dazed**.

Not a moment could be lost—the sheets were ready to go up in flames! I rushed to his washbasin and

---

Tongues of flame darted around The fire was coming very close to

dazed confused

Not a moment could be lost I had to do something right away

pitcher. Luckily, both were filled with water. I lifted them up and **drenched** the bed and Mr. Rochester, then ran back to my room. I grabbed my pitcher and used it on the flames, finally putting them out.

The **hiss of the quenched fire**, the smash of the pitcher as I flung it away, and the splash of water woke Mr. Rochester at last.

"Is there a flood?" he cried, finding himself lying in a pool of water.

"No, sir," I replied, "but there has been a fire. Get up—you are soaked. I'll bring you a candle."

"Is that Jane Eyre?" he demanded, peering at me in the dark. "**Have you plotted** to drown me?"

"Get up, sir!" I begged. "Someone has plotted something. You must find out who and what!"

I fetched the candle from the hallway while he changed into dry clothes. He held up the candle and saw the burned and blackened bed with its wet sheets. The rug was flooded with water.

Then I told him about the strange laugh I had heard, the steps going up to the third floor, and the smell of smoke. He listened without saying a word.

....

drenched wet, soaked
hiss of the quenched fire sound of the fire going out
Have you plotted Did you plan

"Shall I call Mrs. Fairfax?" I asked.

"No! Why would you call her?" he asked. "What can she do?"

"Then I will get Leah, and John and his wife," I said.

"No, let them all sleep," Mr. Rochester insisted. "Stay here for a few minutes. Remain quiet. I must visit the third floor. Don't move, or call anyone."

He left, taking the candle with him. I was now in total darkness. A very long time passed while I waited. Finally, I heard him returning down the hall.

He looked pale and gloomy when he came into the room. "It is as I thought," he said.

"How, sir?"

He made no reply for a while. Then he spoke up. "You heard **an odd** laugh? Have you heard it before?"

"Yes, sir," I said. "A woman who does the sewing here, Grace Poole—she laughs in that odd way."

"Hmm, Grace Poole," Mr. Rochester muttered. "She is, as you say, odd. Well, I shall think things over. Meanwhile, I am glad we are the only ones who know what happened tonight. **Say nothing about it**, Miss

....

an odd a strange

Say nothing about it Do not tell anyone what happened

Eyre. I will explain to the household about the bed. Return to your room. I will sleep on the library sofa."

"Good night, then, sir," I said, turning to go.

"What!" he exclaimed. "You are leaving without **a word of goodwill**? You have saved my life! At least shake hands." He took my hand in both of his and **gazed** at me deeply. "**I can never repay you**, Jane."

"There is no need for that, sir," I said. "I am glad I could help."

"I knew you would do me good in some way, at some time," Mr. Rochester continued. "When I first saw you, your smile and your eyes **struck delight in my heart**." He let my hand go. "Good night!"

I returned to my own room, but could not sleep. Restless and excited, I rose again as soon as dawn came.

....

a word of goodwill allowing me to say something nice
gazed stared
I can never repay you I cannot thank you enough
struck delight in my heart made me feel happy

Chapter Six

A Mystery

I both hoped and feared to see Mr. Rochester the next day. But the morning passed as usual while I taught Adèle her lessons. I did overhear the servants talking near Mr. Rochester's bedroom.

"**What a mercy master** was not burned in his bed!"

"It is always dangerous to keep a candle lit at night."

"How lucky that he had that water jug!"

"And he never woke anyone!"

When I passed his room later, I saw that it had been **scrubbed down**. The burned bed canopies were gone, and Leah was cleaning the smoky windowpanes.

A second person was sitting near the bed, sewing new curtains.

It was Grace Poole.

She looked stiff and silent, as always, and not worried

What a mercy master Master was very lucky that he
scrubbed down cleaned

in the least. I was amazed.

"Good morning, Miss," said Grace.

I decided to test her. "Has anything happened here?" I asked.

"The master was reading in his bed last night," Grace said. "He fell asleep with the candle lit. The bed curtains caught on fire. Luckily, he woke up and **managed** to put out the flames with the water pitcher."

"How strange!" I murmured. I stared at her. "Didn't anyone wake? No one heard him?"

"The servants sleep far away, Miss. Mrs. Fairfax's room is near, but she said she heard nothing." Grace paused and then remarked, "Your room is close, too. **Perhaps** you heard a noise last night?"

"I did," I whispered so Leah would not hear me. "I heard a strange laugh."

Grace calmly continued her sewing. "Master would not laugh if he were in danger. You must have been dreaming."

"I was not dreaming," I insisted.

"Did you open your door and look into the hallway?" she asked.

....

in the least at all
managed was able
Perhaps Maybe, Possibly

I did not want Grace to know I **suspected her**. "Oh, no," I said. "I locked my door. And I will do so from now on."

"A wise thing, Miss," Grace said, and she turned back to her sewing.

For the rest of the day, I **puzzled over** the strange events of the night before. Why didn't Mr. Rochester accuse Grace of setting the fire? And why had he **sworn me to secrecy**?

That evening, Mrs. Fairfax told me that Mr. Rochester had gone to stay with friends. "He will be away a week or more," she said.

Mrs. Fairfax then described the lovely ladies who were likely to be there. She thought Miss Blanche Ingram was the prettiest and the most talented.

When I was alone again, I thought over what Mrs. Fairfax had said. I realized I liked Mr. Rochester more and more each day. Yet I was plain and poor, just a simple governess. Why would he ever have feelings for me?

Ten days passed. Mr. Rochester did not return. Again I reminded myself, "Mr. Rochester **gives you a salary** for teaching Adèle. Be grateful he is kind and

....

suspected her thought she was guilty of something
puzzled over thought about
sworn me to secrecy made me promise not to tell anyone
gives you a salary pays you money

respectful. You must keep any wishes or worries to yourself."

After two weeks, Mrs. Fairfax received a letter from Mr. Rochester. "He is returning in three days with visitors," she said at breakfast. "The rooms must be prepared. The guests will be bringing their maids and valets. We shall have a full house!"

I thought Thornfield Hall was already tidy. But the next three days were busy ones. Extra help was brought in. Servants began to clean, cook, scrub, paint, and polish in a frenzy! Adèle was excited by everything, and ran wild.

During all the **bustle**, I noticed Grace Poole several times. Grace would come out from the third-floor staircase door, wearing a prim cap and a white apron. After checking on the cleaning, she would go down to the kitchen, eat her dinner, and go back to her room.

I found it odd that Grace spent only one hour a day with the other servants. The rest of the time she stayed upstairs alone, sewing on the third floor.

But there was something even odder. No one in the house, except for me, seemed to notice Grace's habits or

....

bustle activity

wonder about them. No one **pitied her loneliness**.

I did overhear Leah and one of the new maids talking one day. "Grace is paid well, I guess?" asked the maid.

"Oh, yes," agreed Leah with a nod. "She understands what she has to do. There's no one who could do her job better—not for all the money she gets."

"That's true!" replied the maid. "I wonder whether the master—"

Just then, Leah noticed me and **gave the other woman a nudge**.

"Doesn't she know?" I heard the new maid whisper.

Leah shook her head, and they stopped talking. The only thing I knew was that there was a mystery at Thornfield. And I was not a part of it.

....

pitied her loneliness felt sorry for her because she spent time alone

gave the other woman a nudge pushed the other woman with her elbow

BEFORE YOU MOVE ON...

1. **Inference** Why does Mr. Rochester say that his candle started the fire?

2. **Conclusions** Reread pages 46 and 51. Jane thinks Grace has something to do with the mystery at Thornfield. Why?

LOOK AHEAD Read to page 65 to find out why Jane may never find happiness with Mr. Rochester.

Chapter Seven

Merry Days
and Noisy Nights

Mr. Rochester returned to Thornfield on a warm spring afternoon. He brought many **elegant** guests with him.

"Bring Adèle to meet the ladies after dinner," Mrs. Fairfax told me.

That evening, I put on my best dress, one of gray silk. Adèle, her hair carefully curled, wore a fancy pink dress. We made our way to the drawing room while the guests were still dining.

When dinner was over, eight ladies **swept** into the room. Some were very tall, and many were dressed in white. I curtsied to them. One or two nodded in return. The others only stared at me.

All the women were beautiful. I spotted Blanche Ingram at once. She was young, with a graceful neck,

---

elegant well-dressed, beautiful
swept walked gracefully

dark eyes, and black hair in ringlets. **Her haughty laugh** was filled with pride.

The young ladies and their mothers **fussed over Adèle**. I sat in a window seat, hoping not to be noticed as the gentlemen entered the room.

I glanced at Mr. Rochester talking with the ladies. The other men were more handsome than Mr. Rochester. But none of them had his soft smile and gentle eyes.

I now knew my true feelings for Mr. Rochester. I was in love.

He soon joined Blanche Ingram by the fireplace. She asked, "Mr. Rochester, where did you find that little Adèle?"

"She was left in my care," Mr. Rochester answered quietly.

"I see you have a governess for her," Miss Ingram said. "**What a nuisance they are!** My sister and I often played tricks on them when we were young."

I stayed only long enough to hear some singing. Then I slipped out to the hall—and ran into Mr. Rochester!

Her haughty laugh Her laugh made her sound superior to others and it

fussed over Adèle competed for Adèle's attention

What a nuisance they are! They are so much trouble!

"Why did you not come and speak with me in the room?" he asked me.

"I did not wish to disturb you, sir."

"You are paler than you used to be," he said. "And you seem sad."

"No, sir. I am simply tired and must go to sleep," I said. **My eyes filled with tears, and I blinked them away.**

"Well, tonight I excuse you," he said. "But as long as the visitors are here, I expect you to appear in the drawing room every evening. Good night, my—" He stopped, bit his lip, and abruptly left.

The days and nights at Thornfield were now merry and noisy, different from my first three months there.

As the days went by, I could tell that Miss Blanche Ingram was falling in love with Mr. Rochester. And he had stopped looking at me.

But I did not feel jealous. Miss Ingram did not impress me. She was not kind, tender, or truthful. And she clearly disliked Adèle. She would push the little girl aside or **order her from** the room.

I guessed Mr. Rochester would marry Blanche

....

My eyes filled with tears, and I blinked them away. I tried not to cry.

order her from tell her to leave

because **of her social connections**. But he did not seem to love her. She was not able to charm him.

And over time, I began to forget his faults. I used to see both the good and bad in him. Now I saw only the good.

One rainy day, Mr. Rochester went to town on business. His guests stayed behind at Thornfield. It was almost dinnertime when we heard a carriage approaching. Then the doorbell rang.

A tall, well-dressed gentleman entered the room. "I understand that my old friend Mr. Rochester is not at home," he said politely. "But I shall wait here till he returns."

The new visitor's name was Richard Mason. He lived in the West Indies, where he had first met Mr. Rochester. His eyes **peered** around blankly as he drew his chair close to the fireplace.

After dinner, a servant told us that a **fortune teller woman** was at the house. She wished to tell **fortunes for the ladies**.

Blanche Ingram went off to have her fortune told.

....

of her social connections she knew many important people
peered looked
fortune teller woman spiritual adviser
fortunes for the ladies the women their future

She did not seem happy when she came back. However, the other young ladies chattered excitedly when they returned.

"She knows all about us!" they shrieked. **"She can read our thoughts!"**

I decided to go to the library myself. The fortune teller sat dressed in a red cloak. A broad-brimmed black hat hid her face.

"You like sitting in a window seat," she said to me. "I know your habits."

"You learned about them from the servants," I said.

"Perhaps I have," she answered. "I do know Mrs. Poole—"

I was **startled** to hear this,

"Don't be alarmed," said the fortune teller. **"There is nothing to fear from her.** But is there someone else you observe in this house? Any of the gentlemen?"

"I don't know the guests," I replied. "And the owner is not at home."

"He is only away for a day or two," the woman said. "You have seen love in his future, have you not?"

So my guesses about him and Blanche Ingram were

"She can read our thoughts!" "She knows what we are thinking!"

startled surprised

There is nothing to fear from her. You should not be afraid of her.

true! "Is Mr. Rochester to be married?" I asked.

"Yes, shortly, and to Miss Ingram," the fortune teller replied. "He must love such a witty lady. And she loves him . . . or at least his money. I spoke with her about that earlier tonight. However, if **another suitor appeared** with more—"

"I want to hear my own fortune, not Mr. Rochester's," I said.

The fortune teller gazed at me for a long time. "You think before you act," she finally said. **"And happiness is within your reach."**

As she talked, the fortune teller's voice and movements changed. They seemed familiar. Then the woman removed her bonnet and said with a smile, "Well, Jane, do you know me?"

It was Mr. Rochester!

"What a strange thing to do!" I said.

"But done well, eh?" he asked.

"Maybe for the other ladies," I said. "But I suspected that you were not really a fortune teller. You have been trying to make me talk nonsense. But I forgive you."

"What are the guests saying about me?" he asked.

....

another suitor appeared she met another man

"And happiness is within your reach." "And you can be happy."

"Discussing the fortune teller, I suppose," I told him. "And **are you aware** that a stranger has arrived today? His name is Mr. Mason, from the West Indies."

Hearing that, he **gripped** my wrist and his smile froze. "Mason! Mason!" he said, his face growing pale. He sat down. "Jane, go to the other room and tell Mason quietly that I am back and wish to see him."

I did as he asked. Much later, after I had gone to bed, I heard Mr. Rochester showing Mr. Mason to a room on the second floor. His voice was calming, and I fell asleep.

Bright moonlight woke me. I rose to close the curtain—and heard a horrible cry that echoed throughout Thornfield Hall. **It died away. My heart stood still.**

The sound had come from the third floor. Now I heard a struggle from above my room. Someone shouted "Help!" three times, then "Rochester!"

I threw on some clothes and dashed into the hall. The guests rushed from their rooms, too, murmuring in confusion.

"Who is hurt?"

....

are you aware did you know

gripped grabbed

It died away. My heart stood still. Now it was quiet. I was scared.

"What has happened?"

"Are there robbers?"

Mr. Rochester came down from the third floor. "It's all right!" he called. "A servant has had a nightmare and thought she saw a ghost. Please return to your rooms. She can't be looked after until the house is **settled**."

I went back to my room and dressed carefully. I wanted to be ready for anything. The noises after the scream had probably been heard only by me. I was certain it was not from a servant's dream. Mr. Rochester must have said that as an excuse, to calm his guests.

An hour went by, and nothing happened. Thornfield Hall was hushed. Then a tap came at my door.

"Are you up and dressed?" It was Mr. Rochester's voice.

"Yes."

"Follow me and make no noise," he said. "Bring a sponge and smelling salts with you."

We glided along the gallery and up the stairs to the dark, low hallway on the third floor. Mr. Rochester stopped in front of one of the small black doors.

....

settled quiet, calm

"**You don't turn sick** at the sight of blood?" he asked me.

"I don't think so," I answered.

He took my hand in his, saying, "I can't risk you fainting." Then he unlocked the door and opened it.

This was one of the rooms Mrs. Fairfax had shown me months before. The large oak bed was surrounded by thick curtains. A looped-up wall tapestry revealed a partly opened door.

A light shone from the inner room. I heard a **snarling** noise, like a dog.

"Wait here," Mr. Rochester said to me, and he went into the inner room.

A laugh greeted him. "Ha! Ha!" I knew that laugh. It was Grace Poole's.

Mr. Rochester soon returned, closing the door behind him.

"Here, Jane!" he said, and I followed him to the other side of the bed. A man, his eyes shut and his head leaning back, sat in a chair. I saw by the candlelight that it was the stranger, Mason. His shirt and arm were soaked in blood.

You don't turn sick Do you get sick
snarling growling

Mr. Rochester used my sponge and the washbasin to clean away some of the blood. Then he waved smelling salts under Mason's nose and woke him up.

"Is there danger?" Mason groaned.

"No, no, just a scratch," said Mr. Rochester. "I'll fetch a doctor. Jane, you must stay here for an hour or two. **Sponge** away the blood when it returns. Use the smelling salts if he feels faint. Do not speak to him for any reason. And, Richard, do not speak to her either."

Mr. Rochester left the room. The key grated in the lock. **His footsteps died** away down the hall.

I did not fear the mysterious third-floor room, or the dark night, or even the blood. But Grace was on the other side of that inner door. I shuddered at the thought of her bursting out.

I waited for what seemed like hours, watching Mason twitch and turn.

My mind raced madly. What had happened? Had Grace stabbed Mason? Why had Mr. Rochester forbidden us to speak?

After two hours or so, Mr. Rochester returned with a doctor.

....

Sponge Wipe

His footsteps died The sound of his footsteps got quieter as he walked

My mind raced madly. I could not stop thinking about everything that had happened.

"I give you half an hour to dress the wound and get the patient downstairs," Mr. Rochester told the doctor. He drew back the window curtains. I was glad to see the dawn.

"I wish I had gotten here sooner," the doctor said, looking at Mason's wound. "He would not have bled so much, perhaps. But what's this? The skin on his shoulder is torn as well as cut. This wound was not done with a knife—there have been teeth here!"

"She bit me," muttered Mason. He shuddered. "I did not expect it. She looked so quiet at first . . ."

"I warned you," Mr. Rochester said. "You should have waited until I went with you. Hurry, Doctor!"

I waited as a lookout by the side door downstairs. Mr. Rochester and the doctor helped Mr. Mason into a waiting carriage. The doctor climbed in, too.

"Let her be taken care of—" Mason began. He burst into tears.

"I will do my best," Mr. Rochester replied. The vehicle drove away. Then he turned to me. "Were you afraid when I left you alone with Mason?"

"I was afraid of someone coming out of the inner

....

I waited as a lookout I had to watch carefully

room," I said.

"But I had locked that door," he said gently. "You were safe."

"Is the danger from last night gone now?" I asked.

"Not until Mason is out of England—and perhaps not even then," Mr. Rochester said bitterly.

He looked closely at my puzzled face. "Now, Jane, let me ask you something. Imagine yourself in a far-off land. You make a mistake, which **will follow you the rest of your life**. Mind you, I'm not talking about a *crime* or anything against the law.

"You return home after twenty years. You **vow** to start your life over. But in order to do this, you must **leap over an obstacle in your way**. Your conscience tells you it's wrong. But should you do it anyway if it will bring you happiness? Is it wrong if you meet a gentle stranger who brings you peace of mind?"

I did not know what to say. Was Blanche Ingram the gentle stranger?

"I have been a restless man," Mr. Rochester said quietly. "But I believe I have found a cure in—"

He paused, and his voice changed. "You have

....

will follow you the rest of your life will affect everything you do

vow promise

leap over an obstacle in your way solve a problem

noticed my feelings for Miss Ingram," he said harshly. "Don't you think if I married her, she could cure me of my restless wanderings?"

He turned and walked away. Then he spun around quickly and came back.

"You are quite pale, Jane," he said to me, taking my hands in his. "What cold fingers! Promise me that you will sit up with me on the night before I am married? I can talk to you about my lovely bride, for you seem to know her well."

Then he **strode** away. I heard him cheerily greet two of the guests. "Mason was up before all of you. He left before sunrise; I saw him **off** myself."

....

strode walked confidently
off leave

BEFORE YOU MOVE ON...

1. **Conflict** What are Jane's feelings toward Mr. Rochester? What obstacles might stand in the way of her feelings?

2. **Summarize** What happens to Mr. Mason on his visit to Thornfield?

LOOK AHEAD Read pages 66–72 to learn about Jane's painful decision.

Chapter Eight

A Reunion with Aunt Reed

On the following day, a message came from Gateshead Hall. My cousin John Reed had died! And my aunt had had a stroke. Now she wanted to see me.

I had never liked my cousin. Yet the news of his death was still awful!

I went to ask Mr. Rochester **for some time off**. "If you please, sir, I must leave for a week or two. My aunt—Mrs. Reed of Gateshead—has sent for me," I said.

Mr. Rochester nodded. "You'll need money to travel," he said. He gave me some of the salary I was owed.

"There is something else, sir," I added. I paused and took a deep breath. "**Apparently**, you are to be married. In that case, Adèle ought to go away to school."

....

for some time off if I could leave my job for a few days
Apparently Clearly

"To get her out of my bride's way, I suppose," Mr. Rochester said. "Yes, it makes sense."

"And I will **advertise for another position as governess**," I said.

"What?" he exclaimed.

I nodded firmly. I could not **bear the idea of** staying at Thornfield after Mr. Rochester married Blanche. "Both Adèle and I must be safely out of the house before your bride enters it," I said.

With that, I left for Gateshead.

The Reeds' house looked the same as I remembered. But the people had changed greatly. Cousin Eliza was now tall and thin. She wore a plain black dress. Her sister, Georgiana, was very plump, with yellow hair in ringlets. Her dress was also black, but fashionable.

"Hello, Miss Eyre," they coolly greeted me. They did not want me to see their mother, saying she was too tired.

But I had not traveled a hundred miles only to be kept away. I went to see my aunt. She lay in bed on a pile of pillows. I **stooped** and kissed her.

....

advertise for another position as governess make an announcement that you need a new teacher

bear the idea of think about

stooped knelt; bent over

I could not forget the terrors of my childhood. I had vowed as a child to never call her aunt again. Now I felt sadness for her suffering and was ready to forgive and forget.

"Is this Jane Eyre?" she asked.

"Yes, Aunt Reed," I replied. "How are you, dear aunt? You sent for me."

"Such a **burden** that child was!" Aunt Reed mumbled, her eyes closed. "And sickly! My husband paid more attention to it than to his own children."

Aunt Reed opened her eyes and looked at me from her bed.

"**Twice I have done you a wrong**," she muttered. "One was breaking the promise I made to my husband to **bring you up** as my own child. The other—" she tried to turn slightly but could not.

"Go to my dresser and take out the letter you'll find there," she ordered me.

I obeyed her.

"Read the letter," she said.

....

burden problem, bother

Twice I have done you a wrong I have done two bad things to you

bring you up take care of you

Madam,

Will you kindly send me the address of my niece, Jane Eyre, and tell me how she is. I intend to ask her to come to me at Madeira. I am unmarried and have no children. Therefore, I wish to adopt her and leave her my possessions at the time of my death.

Sincerely,
John Eyre

The writer was my uncle! But the letter's date was three years ago.

"Why did I never hear of this letter from my uncle John?" I asked.

"I did not want to help you," my aunt confessed. "I never forgot your voice when you said you hated me."

"Please forgive me for what I said years ago," I said. "I was only a child."

"Well, I **took my revenge**," said my aunt weakly. "I wrote to your uncle and told him you had died from fever at Lowood School. If you wish, write and tell him I lied."

....

took my revenge tried to hurt you because you hurt me

"Aunt, think no more about it," I begged her. "Look at me with kindness now. I **long** to be forgiven, as I forgive you for the way you treated me."

But Mrs. Reed would not. Poor woman, to still hate me after so many years! She fell into a **stupor** and was dead by midnight.

I stayed at Gateshead for a month to help out. Then I returned to Thornfield.

During the long journey back, I **mulled over** news I had received from Mrs. Fairfax. The houseguests had finally left and Mr. Rochester had gone to London to buy a new carriage. No doubt he was making wedding plans.

I walked up the road from town on a mild June evening. I felt glad to be going home to Thornfield. But I had to remind myself that it was not really my home at all. In a few weeks, or even days, I would have to **move on**.

Near the house, I spied Mr. Rochester. He sat on a stone step, writing in a book. My heart beat wildly.

"Jane Eyre!" he exclaimed when he saw me. "You've

....

long want
stupor deep sleep
mulled over thought about the
move on find somewhere else to live

been gone from home a whole month—and have forgotten me, I'm sure."

His words thrilled me. He was worried that I might have forgotten him! And he spoke of Thornfield as my home!

"Mrs. Fairfax wrote to me about your errand to London," I said boldly.

"So you know about my new carriage!" he replied. "I think it will **suit my bride**. Now hurry home, Jane, and rest your feet."

I had no ready answer. His words confused me. How much *did* he care for me?

I meant to walk away calmly. Instead, I suddenly exclaimed, "Thank you for your kindness. Wherever *you* are is my home—my only home."

I turned away and hurried to the house. How embarrassed I was! Why had I said such a thing?

Mrs. Fairfax and Adèle were happy to see me. Even Leah and Sophie seemed pleased at my return.

For the next two weeks, nothing more was said of Mr. Rochester's wedding. I saw no other preparations being made.

....

suit my bride make my bride happy
I had no ready answer. I did not know what to say.

And Mr. Rochester paid no visits to Blanche Ingram's house. I began to wonder if the marriage to her would happen. **Had they changed their minds?**

I stopped worrying about leaving Thornfield. Perhaps things would be fine after all.

Mr. Rochester seemed **content** as the days went by. He had never been kinder to me. And I had never loved him more.

Had they changed their minds? Did they decide not to get married?

content happy

BEFORE YOU MOVE ON...

1. **Conclusions** Reread pages 66–67. Why does Jane decide to leave Thornfield?

2. **Character's Point of View** Reread pages 67–70. Why is Jane able to forgive her aunt?

LOOK AHEAD Read pages 73–80 to see what Mr. Rochester's true feelings are.

Chapter Nine

An Unexpected Proposal

By midsummer, the skies were blue and sunny, and the mowed fields around Thornfield were green. One June evening, I went out to the garden. It was filled with the sweet smells of flowers. And there was another scent as well. It was Mr. Rochester's cigar.

I saw Mr. Rochester enter the garden, and we began to walk together. We sat down on a bench under a large chestnut tree.

"I see you like Thornfield," he said.

"Yes, indeed," I replied.

"You will be sorry to **part** from little Adèle and Mrs. Fairfax?" he asked. He gazed at me with his dark, **brooding** eyes.

I hesitated. "Yes," I answered sadly. "Must I move on, sir? Must I leave Thornfield?"

"I'm sorry, Jane, but you must."

....

part move away
brooding angry

I said nothing. **My hopes were dashed!**

"I am to be married soon, you know," Mr. Rochester continued. "You'll remember I planned to take beautiful Blanche Ingram as my wife. So Adèle must go away to school. And you must find a new position."

"Yes, sir," I said, my voice shaking.

"I have heard about a job for you in Ireland," Mr. Rochester remarked.

"Ireland is a long way off, sir," I said. "And the sea **is a barrier** . . . from England and from Thornfield and—"

"Well?" Mr. Rochester asked.

"And from *you*, sir." With that, I began to weep quietly. "It **strikes me with terror to be torn** from you because of your bride!"

"What bride? I have no bride!" Mr. Rochester exclaimed.

"But you will," I sobbed.

"Yes, I will!" he said firmly. "And you must stay!"

"I tell you I must go!" I cried. "How can I stay here? Am I a machine without feelings? I may be poor and plain. But I have as much soul and heart as you! We

---

My hopes were dashed! I lost hope because I did not want to leave Thornfield!

is a barrier blocks my way

strikes me with terror to be torn makes me afraid to be away

are equals!"

"Yes, Jane, we are!" Mr. Rochester declared. He tried to gather me in his arms.

"And yet we are not equals!" I said, pulling away. "For you are to wed Miss Ingram. I do not believe you truly love her. I would never marry someone I do not love—therefore I am better than you!"

He shook his head and tried to embrace me again.

I struggled in his arms. "Let me go!" I cried. "I'll go to Ireland! I have **spoken my mind** and can go anywhere now!"

"No, Jane!" pleaded Mr. Rochester. "I offer you my heart, my hand, and a share of everything I own. Come to me."

"You tease me," I said scornfully.

"No, Jane, it is *you* I **intend** to marry," he said, drawing me close. "**My bride is *here* because my equal is here.** Jane, will you marry me?"

I could not answer. Was he mocking me?

"I only pretended to you that I wished to marry Miss Ingram," he said. "I wanted you to be as madly in love with me as I am with you. I knew you would be

....

spoken my mind told you how I feel

intend plan

My bride is *here* because my equal is here. I want you as my bride because I see you as my equal.

jealous of her."

I looked at him. "Did you think of *her* feelings, sir?"

"Her feelings are only of pride," Mr. Rochester said firmly. "It will not hurt her to be humbled." His face was flushed. "Please, Jane, I swear I love you, truly!"

I knew he was **sincere**. "Then I will marry you, dear Edward!" I cried.

We sat holding each other for a while. I had never felt so happy! The nightmare of leaving Thornfield had changed into something wonderful.

The wind began to roar, and the chestnut tree shook and groaned. There was a sudden crack of lightning and a crash of thunder, and a **torrent** of rain fell.

Mr. Rochester hurried me across the grounds to the house. Neither of us saw Mrs. Fairfax come out of her room as we stood dripping in the hall.

"Good night, my darling," he said to me with a kiss. When I looked up, there was a pale and amazed Mrs. Fairfax. But I could not worry about Mrs. Fairfax. I was too joyful!

The storm raged through the night. Though I was alone in my room, I was not afraid.

....

sincere truthful, honest
torrent shower

The next morning, little Adèle came running in. She told me that the chestnut tree had been struck by lightning in the night and had split in half.

The next morning, Mr. Rochester told me his plans. Our wedding would take place quietly in four weeks, in the church near Thornfield. Then we would travel through France and Italy.

Mr. Rochester insisted that I choose some new dresses for myself in town. He also wanted to give me jewelry that had belonged to his family. But I refused the jewelry. It did not seem right for me to wear such fancy things.

I asked Mr. Rochester to tell Mrs. Fairfax about our wedding plans. I hurried to her parlor after he had spoken with her.

"You are so young," she began. "I **daresay** Mr. Rochester is fond of you. I hope all will be good. But you cannot be too careful. Gentlemen like him do not tend to marry their governesses."

Why was she saying such things? Luckily, the shopping trip kept me too busy to worry.

---

daresay believe

Mr. Rochester wanted me to pick six dresses. I only wanted two. He selected a purple silk and a pink satin. I knew I would never wear such bright dresses. So I picked two others instead: one of black satin and one of gray silk.

The more he bought me that day, the worse I felt. On the trip back to Thornfield, I suddenly remembered the letter that John Eyre had sent to my aunt Reed.

It would be a relief to have a little money of my own. **I could not bear to be showered with presents by** Mr. Rochester.

I wrote to my uncle John that very day and told him I was to be married soon.

If one day I can bring money to Mr. Rochester, it will not seem so terrible to take his gifts now, I thought.

I also vowed to continue as Adèle's governess and to buy my own clothes out of my salary.

The four weeks passed quickly. My trunks were packed and locked, ready to be sent to London. My wedding dress and veil hung in the closet of my room.

All seemed settled. Then something strange happened two nights before our wedding.

....

I could not bear to be showered with presents by I did not want to receive a lot of gifts from

The wind blew harshly that night. I dreamed that Thornfield was **a ruin**. Only bats and owls lived in it. I tried to climb the wall around the house and fell.

That woke me. I saw a **gleam** of candlelight on the dresser. My closet door stood open, and I heard a rustling from inside. Perhaps it was Adèle's nurse, Sophie.

A woman came out, holding my wedding gown and veil. "Sophie, what are you doing?" I asked. She was silent.

I rose up in my bed and bent forward to look at her. **My blood ran cold.** It was not Sophie, or Leah, or Mrs. Fairfax. It was not even Grace Poole.

I had never seen the woman before. She was tall and large, with long, dark hair. I could not tell if her clothing was a dress or a sheet. Throwing my veil over her head, she looked in the mirror.

I saw her face. The eyes were red and bloodshot, the face almost purple. She reminded me of a vampire!

As I watched in fear, she took my veil off her head and tore it in half. Then she flung the pieces down and **trampled** on them.

Dawn was coming, and the strange creature sensed

....

a ruin destroyed
gleam flash, twinkle
My blood ran cold. I was very scared.
trampled stamped her feet

it. She came over and glared down at me, putting out her candle. **I lost consciousness from terror.** When I woke, the creature was gone.

The next day, I told Mr. Rochester. "You must have dreamed it," he insisted.

"But when I woke this morning, I saw my veil in two pieces on the carpet!" I said.

Mr. Rochester threw his arms around me. "I am glad only the veil was hurt, and not you!" he exclaimed. "The woman must have been Grace Poole. You know how strange she is, Jane. Remember what she did to me? To Mason? You were half-asleep, and perhaps **feverish**. No wonder she looked different to you."

He added, "You wonder why I keep such a woman in my house. When we have been married a year and a day, I will tell you. But not now."

I was not completely satisfied with his explanation. But who else could the vampire woman have been? I went to bed that night but hardly slept at all.

....

I lost consciousness from terror. I was so scared that I fainted.

feverish sick

BEFORE YOU MOVE ON...

1. **Plot** How does Mr. Rochester convince Jane that he loves her?

2. **Foreshadowing** Reread pages 76–80. What shows that Jane's and Mr. Rochester's plan to marry might not work?

LOOK AHEAD Read pages 81–90 to see what happens at Jane's wedding.

Chapter Ten

A Mystery Revealed

The next morning, Mr. Rochester and I walked **briskly** to church for our wedding. He grasped my hand as we hurried along. His face was **grim and determined**. Did all grooms look that way before their wedding?

There were no bridesmaids or ushers. Only the clergyman, Mr. Wood, and his clerk waited for us. Two people slipped into the shadows from a side door. I supposed they wished to **witness** the ceremony.

The service began. Mr. Wood explained the intent of marriage. Then he said to us, "If you know of any reason why you should not be married, confess it now."

He paused. Then a man's voice spoke from behind us. "The marriage cannot go on. I declare an obstacle."

Without turning his head, Mr. Rochester said, "**Proceed** with the ceremony, Mr. Wood."

"This wedding cannot proceed. Mr. Rochester

....

briskly quickly

grim and determined gloomy and serious

witness watch, observe

Proceed Go on; Continue

already has a wife," the speaker said calmly.

I felt shaken and cold. Mr. Rochester put his arm around me. "Who are you?" he asked the man.

"My name is Briggs. I am a lawyer from London. I am here to remind you **of your wife**."

Mr. Rochester's eyes **glittered coldly**. "Then give me proof. Tell me her name and where she lives."

"Certainly," Mr. Briggs said. He took a document from his pocket and read:

> *Fifteen years ago, Edward Rochester of Thornfield Hall was married to my sister, Bertha Mason, at a church in Jamaica, West Indies. The record of that marriage will be found at the church. I have a copy of it as well.*
>
> *Richard Mason*

"That document may **prove** I have been married," said Mr. Rochester. "But it does not prove that the woman is still living."

"She was living three months ago," said Mr. Briggs. "And here is a witness."

---

of your wife that you are already married
glittered coldly looked very angry
prove show

The second stranger stepped forward. It was Richard Mason! Mr. Rochester glared at him and asked, "What have *you* to say?"

"His wife is now at Thornfield Hall," Mason said to Mr. Wood. "I saw her there last April. I am her brother."

The clergyman looked astonished. "Impossible! I have lived in this neighborhood for years. I never heard of a Mrs. Rochester at Thornfield."

Mr. Rochester smiled grimly. "**I took care that none should hear of her,**" he muttered. He thought for a few minutes. Then he announced, "There shall be no wedding today! What this lawyer says is true."

He turned to Mr. Wood and added, "Perhaps you have heard gossip about **a madwoman** at Thornfield. I now tell you that she is my wife, who is mad. Like her mother, she turned out to be a maniac. I invite you all to the house to visit Mrs. Poole's patient—*my wife!*"

He looked over at me. "Jane knew nothing of my secret," he added. "She thought all was fair and legal in marrying me. Come, all of you!"

Back at the house, Mr. Rochester **gruffly brushed off** people waiting to greet us. Holding my hand tightly,

....

I took care that none should hear of her I made sure that no one would know I had a wife

a madwoman an insane woman

gruffly brushed off rudely ignored

he climbed the stairs to the third floor. The three gentlemen followed us into the room where Mason had been attacked.

Mr. Rochester lifted the tapestry and unlocked the inner door. Inside that room, a lamp hung from the ceiling. Grace Poole bent over a fireplace, cooking something in a saucepan.

And at the far end of the room, a figure ran back and forth on **all fours**. It growled like a wild animal, and dark hair hid its face.

"Good morning, Mrs. Poole!" said Mr. Rochester. "How are you? And how is your **charge** today?"

"We're well, sir," replied Grace.

At those words, the creature rose up and stood on its **hind** feet.

"Ah, sir, she sees you!" exclaimed Grace. "You'd better not stay."

The maniac yelled and parted her shaggy hair. I knew that purple face. It was the one I had seen in my room two nights before!

"Beware!" Grace suddenly screamed. Mason and the others stepped back. Mr. Rochester flung me behind

....

all fours their hands and knees

charge patient

hind back

him just as the maniac **sprang** for his throat.

The two of them wrestled fiercely, her teeth on his cheek. At last he managed to tie her to a chair.

"Compare this wife of mine and this young woman!" Mr. Rochester said, putting his hand on my shoulder. **"Then judge me if you will!"**

We all left the room, but Mr. Rochester stayed behind to give an order to Grace Poole. The lawyer spoke as we went downstairs.

"You are cleared from all blame," Mr. Briggs said to me. "If your uncle John Eyre is still living, he will be glad to hear it."

"My uncle?" I said in amazement. How could this lawyer—a stranger to me—know of my uncle?

"Mr. Mason knows him," explained Mr. Briggs. "When your uncle received your letter about your plans to marry, Mr. Mason told him the truth about Rochester. Sadly, John Eyre was very ill in Madeira and could not come rescue you. So he asked Mr. Mason to prevent the false marriage. You had better remain in England until you hear more from me or your uncle."

Once the men had left, I went to my room, locked

....

sprang jumped

"Then judge me if you will!" "Then tell me I made the wrong decision if you want!"

You are cleared from all blame You have done nothing wrong

the door, and took off my wedding dress. I was too tired to even weep.

I had almost been a bride, but now I was a lonely young woman again. Mr. Rochester was not the man I thought he was. There was only one thing to do—I had to leave him and Thornfield.

Later in the day, dizzy and faint, I opened my door. Mr. Rochester was waiting in the hall. He brought me down to the library and gave me some food and drink.

"I was wrong to ever bring you to Thornfield Hall, knowing how it was haunted," he said to me. "I do have another house, Ferndean Manor. But it is an unhealthy and **isolated** place. I would not keep my mad wife there."

He paced the room. "I'll pay Grace Poole more to live here alone with my wife, **boarded up**."

"You are cruel, sir!" I interrupted him. "Your wife cannot help her madness."

"You don't understand!" Mr. Rochester exclaimed. "In any case, I ask that you spend just one more night **under this roof**, Jane. Then I will take you to the south of France, where we will live together for always."

....

isolated lonely
boarded up locked in this room
under this roof in this house

I knew I could not do that. I could not live with a man who was married to another woman. But I listened to all Mr. Rochester had to say. He told me how his father had arranged the marriage between him and Bertha Mason. Her father had been very wealthy.

"She was beautiful. I was young, and thought I loved her," Mr. Rochester explained. "Her family **encouraged our match**. So did my father and brother.

"After the honeymoon, I learned that my bride's mother was not dead—but mad! She and another brother of Bertha's were locked up in **an asylum**. Richard Mason himself will probably go mad one day. My father and brother knew all this. But they thought only of the money that Bertha would **inherit**, and they joined in the plot against me.

"Jane, I lived with that woman for four years in the West Indies. I soon found her to be completely different from me. We had nothing to say to each other. At first she was **coarse** and stupid, but she soon became worse. It wasn't long before the doctors discovered she was mad. My father and brother had both died by then. And I had inherited Thornfield."

....

encouraged our match wanted us to get married

an asylum a mental hospital

inherit receive from her parents when they died

coarse rude

"What did you do?" I asked him.

"I decided to move with Bertha to England, where no one knew we were married. I placed her in safety and comfort, and kept her a secret. She has now been at Thornfield for ten years. Only Grace and the doctor—who bandaged Mason—know. Mrs. Fairfax and the other servants may have suspected something, but they did not know the complete truth for sure.

"Bertha has escaped three times. Once she tried to burn me in my bed. Once she attacked her brother, Richard. And finally she paid that **ghastly** visit to you and tore your wedding veil."

Mr. Rochester then told me how he had looked everywhere for a good and intelligent woman to love. He had hoped he'd be able to find one who would understand his sad situation.

For ten long years he'd searched throughout Europe. But he hadn't met the right woman. So he'd come back to England.

"And it was here at Thornfield that I met you," he said **earnestly** to me. "I saw how gentle and good you

---

ghastly awful
earnestly eagerly

were, how bright and independent. I fell in love and resolved to marry you."

I was filled with love for him. Yet I knew what had to be done. "Mr. Rochester, I can*not* be yours," I said. "We must go our separate ways. I am sure you will forget me before I can forget you."

Mr. Rochester was furious. He angrily **seized** my arm. "You are going? You are leaving me?"

"Yes," I replied, tears stinging my eyes. "God bless you and keep you from harm." And as I left the room, **my heart cried** *farewell*!

Early the next morning, I rose from bed. I took my purse with the only money I had, and a locket, a ring, and some linen.

I softly glided past Mrs. Fairfax's door, then Adèle's. I heard Mr. Rochester pacing in his room. Down in the kitchen I got some water and bread. I quietly unlocked the door and walked out of the house.

Dawn glimmered in the yard. I slipped through the gates and headed down the road, away from

....

seized grabbed
my heart cried *farewell* it was painful to leave
Dawn glimmered in the yard. The sun was beginning to rise.

Thornfield.

I did not know where I was going. But I did not look back.

BEFORE YOU MOVE ON...

1. **Summarize** Reread pages 81–83. Explain why Jane and Mr. Rochester do not get married.

2. **Plot** Mr. Rochester wants to move to France with Jane. Why does Jane refuse?

LOOK AHEAD Read pages 91–103 to find out how Jane's life changes when she leaves Thornfield.

Chapter Eleven

On My Own

For two days, I traveled by coach **as far as my money could take me**. When the coach dropped me **at a deserted crossroads**, I forgot to take my **parcel** with me. So then I had nothing.

What was I to do? The day was hot. I struggled to a village and entered a bakery shop. But I had no money to buy bread.

"Do you know of any place where a servant or dressmaker is needed?" I asked wearily. The clerk shook her head.

Exhausted and starving, I wandered for hours. A little before dark, I begged a piece of bread from a local farmer. To my surprise, he gave me a thick slice.

I spent the night in nearby woods, on the cold, damp ground. It rained the next day. I had no shelter. Soaked to the skin, I looked for work and food again.

....

as far as my money could take me for as long as I had money to pay the driver

at a deserted crossroads on an empty street

parcel package

At one cottage door, a little girl was tossing cold porridge into a pig trough.

"Will you give me that?" I asked her.

She stared at me. "Mother!" she called. "A woman wants this porridge."

"Well, lass, give it to the beggar," replied a woman from indoors. "The pig doesn't want it."

The girl emptied the **stiff mass** into my hands, and I ate it hungrily.

Twilight came, and I wandered far away from the village. Among the rainy marshes, I spied a light in the distance. I walked toward it over a hill, across a wide **bog**, and up a road.

Finally I reached a house. The friendly light shone from a low window. Bending down, I peered inside. An elderly woman sat knitting in the kitchen while two younger ones read.

I listened to their quiet talk. The two young women were sisters, Diana and Mary Rivers. They were waiting for the return of their brother, St. John. The older woman was a servant named Hannah.

Perhaps they could help me. I **timidly** knocked at

....

stiff mass dry, hard cereal
Twilight came It started to get dark
bog swamp
timidly shyly

the door, and Hannah opened it.

"May I speak to the young ladies?" I asked. "I need shelter for the night and a morsel of bread to eat."

Hannah looked at me suspiciously. "I'll give you a piece of bread," she said. "But we can't take in a **vagrant**. Here is a penny; now please go."

Worn out, I sank down on the step and wept as the door shut. Just then, a person appeared near me, knocking at the door.

"St. John, how wet and cold you must be!" exclaimed Hannah. "Come in—there has been a beggar here. Why, here she is still!"

"I overheard your conversation with her," St. John said. "I will speak with the woman." He asked me to come in.

His sister Diana kindly gave me bread and milk, which I ate **feebly**. I told her my name was Jane Elliott. I did not want anyone to know who I really was.

"And where do you live? Where are your friends?" Mary asked.

"What has happened to you?" St. John added.

"Sir, I can give you no details tonight," I said

....

vagrant homeless person, beggar
feebly weakly

weakly. "But I will trust you. If I were a stray dog, I know you would not turn me away."

I was right to trust them. Soon I was taken upstairs to a warm, dry bed, and gratefully fell asleep.

For three days and nights I lay in bed, barely moving and not speaking at all. I heard Diana and Mary whispering, "It is good we took her in" and "She has **gone through strange hardships**."

On the fourth day, I was able to speak and move. Hannah brought me **gruel** and dry toast to eat.

My clothes, cleaned and dried, were on a chair by the bed. I slowly dressed and went downstairs to the kitchen.

From talking to Hannah, I learned that St. John Rivers was a **parson** who lived a few miles away. His sisters were both governesses.

The family took me into the parlor, where the pretty sisters fussed over me. But St. John did not speak until tea was served. He was in his late twenties, tall and slender with large blue eyes.

"If you'll tell us where your friends live, we can

....

gone through strange hardships experienced unusual problems

gruel a thick mixture of water and corn meal

parson man who worked for the church

write to them and return you home," he said kindly.

"I have no home or friends," I said.

"You have never been married?" St. John asked.

"No," I said. My face burned. I added, "I *can* tell you that I am an orphan. I spent six years as a student at Lowood School, and two more as a teacher. I became a governess nearly a year ago. I had to leave four days before you found me here. It would be useless and dangerous to explain why I left. But I am free of blame. And I am grateful to you three for taking me in."

"You said your name was Jane Elliott?" St. John asked me.

"I did, but it is not my real name. Yet I wish to be called that for now," I said. "Help me **seek** work. Then I will leave."

St. John promised he would try.

The more time I stayed with them, the more I liked Mary and Diana. I read books and **sketched. Days passed like hours, and weeks passed like days.**

When a month had gone by, Diana and Mary prepared to return to their jobs. St. John told me that he had found work for me. Would I be the teacher at a new

---

seek look for

sketched drew pictures

Days passed like hours, and weeks passed like days. The time passed very quickly.

school for girls? The school even had a little cottage for me to live in! I was happy to **accept the offer**.

The day before I was to move to town, a letter came for St. John.

"Our uncle John is dead," he said to his sisters. He showed them the letter. They all smiled sadly.

"We never knew our mother's brother," Diana explained to me. "He died with a fortune of twenty thousand pounds. He did not have a wife or children— we and one other person were his only relatives.

"We hoped we would inherit some of the money. But this letter says that he has left it to the other **relation**."

St. John locked the letter in his desk. He and his sisters did not speak again about it. And in a few days, each of us went our separate ways.

....

accept the offer take the job
relation relative

Chapter Twelve

A Fresh Start

The new school opened with twenty poor students. Only three knew how to read. None could write or add. **I was saddened by the girls' ignorance and bad manners.** Yet I knew I could teach them and help them.

When the first day of school was over, St. John paid a visit to my little cottage. He handed me a present from his sisters. The parcel contained a paint box, colored pencils, and paper.

"Is the teaching harder than you expected?" he asked.

"Oh, no!" I replied. "I think I will do well here. I am content to work at it."

"We each have the power over our own fate," St. John remarked.

As the weeks went by, I wondered if I had made

....

I was saddened by the girls' ignorance and bad manners.
I felt sad because the girls did not know very much and were rude.

We each have the power over our own fate We all have control over our own lives

the right choice. People in the town greeted me with friendly smiles. I was thankful for all I now had.

Yet no one would ever love me as Edward Rochester had. Perhaps I should have gone away with him. But I would have felt **regret and shame**. I was truly better off as a village schoolteacher, free and honest.

One day, St. John brought a poetry book to my cottage. I had been busy painting, but I stopped to look at the poems.

I saw St. John peer at my painting. Next to it was a sheet of thin paper. I liked to rest my hand on it while working, in order to keep the painted cardboard clean. St. John moved the thin paper over the painting to protect it. Then something must have **caught his eye**.

I did not know what he suddenly saw on the blank piece of paper. He **snatched it up**, looked at it closely, then glanced over at me.

"What is the matter?" I asked.

"Nothing at all," he replied, putting down the paper. I saw him neatly tear a narrow piece from the edge. He stuck it in his glove, nodded good-bye, and quickly left the cottage.

----

regret and shame sorry later and embarrassed
caught his eye made him look
snatched it up grabbed it

Once he was gone, I examined the paper. But I saw nothing on it, except for some traces of paint and pencil.

"Whatever he saw could not have been too important," I decided. And I soon forgot **about the incident**.

It had begun to snow when St. John left my cottage that night, and it continued to snow. By the following night, heavy **drifts** lay everywhere. The wind howled outside my snug rooms.

I heard a noise at the door. But it was not the wind. St. John unlatched the door and came in.

I was startled to have a visitor. "Has anything happened?" I asked.

"No," he answered, stamping the snow from his boots. "I want to have a little talk with you."

He sat down and stared at the glowing fire while we chatted about his sisters and my students. Then he suddenly stood up and turned to me.

"I have a **tale** to tell you," he said. "Perhaps it will not sound new or fresh. **But hear me out.**

"Twenty years ago, a poor parson married a rich

....

about the incident that it had happened
drifts piles of snow
tale story
But hear me out. Please listen to me.

man's daughter. Sadly, in less than two years the couple died. They left a little daughter, who was cared for by the rich relatives. She was raised by an aunt, a Mrs. Reed of Gateshead."

I gave a quiet gasp. But St. John continued with his story,

"Mrs. Reed kept the orphan for ten years. I do not know whether the child was happy there or not. But at the end of that time, Mrs. Reed sent her to Lowood School. That is where you were, is it not?

"After being a pupil there, she became a teacher— just like you. She left the school to be a governess— again, how similar to you! Her **task** was to educate the ward of a Mr. Rochester."

"Mr. Rivers!" I interrupted.

"My story is almost done," he said. "All I know about Mr. Rochester is that he proposed marriage to the governess. But she found out he had a wife already, who was **a lunatic**.

"The governess fled Thornfield Hall in the night. No one has located her. But it is now **urgent** that she be found. Advertisements have been put in the newspapers.

....

I gave a quiet gasp. I took a deep breath.

task job

a lunatic an insane person

urgent very important

I myself have just received a letter about all this from a lawyer, Mr. Briggs. Is it not an odd tale?"

"Since you know so much, tell me this," I pleaded. "How is Mr. Rochester?"

"I do not know," St. John replied. "Mr. Briggs wrote to him, but the reply he got back was from a Mrs. Fairfax."

My heart sank. Mr. Rochester must have fled Thornfield.

"Since you did not ask me the governess's name, I will tell you," St. John said. "Or rather, I will show you." He took a slip of torn paper from his pocket. It was the same piece he had taken from my desk the day before.

Among the streaks of colored paint on it were the words JANE EYRE . . . in my own handwriting. I must have scribbled them down while **daydreaming**.

"You are Jane Eyre and not Jane Elliott?" St. John asked me.

"Yes, yes," I admitted. "But—"

"You have not asked why Mr. Briggs is seeking you," St. John said. "It is to tell you that your uncle,

....

My heart sank. I was very sad.

daydreaming thinking about something else

Mr. John Eyre of Madeira, is dead. Mr. Eyre left you all his **property**, and you are now rich."

I could hardly believe what he was saying. "I—rich?"

"Yes, quite. You are worth twenty thousand pounds."

I was even more amazed. It was so much money! But something else puzzled me greatly.

"Why did Mr. Briggs write to you about me?" I asked. "How did he know you? Why would he think you could help him in his search?"

St. John looked embarrassed. He did not want to tell me the reason. But I insisted. Then, to my astonishment, he told me the following.

"My mother's **maiden** name was Eyre," St. John said. "One of her brothers, a clergyman, married Miss Jane Reed. That was your mother. My mother's other brother was John Eyre, who lived in Madeira."

I thought about all he had just told me. "So your mother was one of my aunts?"

St. John nodded. "Yes. Diana, Mary, and I are your cousins."

---

property land and money
maiden family name; given name

What a discovery! I felt rich twice. Not only did I have money, but now I had kind and loving relatives— relatives who had rescued me on their doorstep. How lucky I was, and how very glad!

I had grown to love Mary and Diana and to respect St. John. "Twenty thousand pounds is more than I could ever need," I said. "I want to share the money with you and your sisters. We will each inherit five thousand pounds that way."

St. John did not want to take my money, though I insisted on it. When they heard the whole story, his sisters also argued against **my wishes**. But in the end I **won the battle** and shared the fortune equally with my three cousins.

....

my wishes what I wanted to do

won the battle convinced them

BEFORE YOU MOVE ON...

1. **Comparisons** How is Jane's life as a school teacher different from the life she would have with Mr. Rochester?

2. **Character** Jane shares her fortune with her cousins. What does this say about her?

LOOK AHEAD Read pages 104–115 to find out if Jane is happy as a rich woman.

Chapter Thirteen

Return to Thornfield

Everything was settled by Christmas. Diana and Mary were leaving their jobs as governesses. We would live together in their family's house, where they had taken me in. Before their arrival, I cleaned the **place from top to bottom** with Hannah's help.

New carpets and curtains gave the old house a fresh, cheerful look. When Mary and Diana finally appeared, they were delighted with everything.

For a week, the sisters and I enjoyed ourselves **mightily**! We were **giddy** from the fresh air, the comforts of our home, and our newfound riches. We then settled down to our usual habits of reading, studying, and talking.

I still taught the students at the village school, but only once a week. The girls had turned out to be **respectable and well-informed**.

....

place from top to bottom entire house
mightily very much
giddy happy, excited
respectable and well-informed honest and smart

You may wonder if I had forgotten Mr. Rochester, now that my fortunes had changed. Not at all! I longed to know how he was and what he was doing.

So I wrote to Mrs. Fairfax at Thornfield Hall. Two months went by, and there was no reply. I wrote to her again. Months passed, and still I heard nothing.

I could not enjoy the spring. Even the start of summer held no joy for me.

Then one Monday night, an odd thing happened. St. John and I were talking after everyone else had gone to bed. The candle was almost burned out, and moonlight filled the room.

Suddenly my heart seemed to stop. A sharp, strange thrill passed through my head and limbs.

St. John noticed that something was wrong. "What do you hear? What do you see?" he asked.

I saw nothing. But I heard a voice somewhere cry painfully, "Jane! Jane! Jane!" It did not seem to be in the room, or the house, or the garden. But I knew—and loved—that voice well.

It was Edward Rochester's. **He was calling to me across the months and the miles.** "I am coming!"

....

Suddenly my heart seemed to stop.   Without warning, I felt very nervous and excited.

He was calling to me across the months and miles. I could hear him in my memory.

I called back with a gasp. "Wait for me!"

My path was now clear. I would seek out Edward Rochester, wherever he might be!

The next morning, I told Diana and Mary that I had to go away for a few days. In the early June afternoon, I waited for a coach at the crossroads. It was the same coach I had stepped from nearly a year earlier, lonely and fearful.

The journey to Thornfield took a day and a half. I got out at **an inn** two miles from the house and set out the rest of the way on foot.

He may not even be in England, for all you know, I reminded myself as I walked across the fields. *And if he is there, so is his wife . . .*

I hurried on anyway. Finally I could see the gates in the distance. The house was hidden. I decided to approach the house from the front.

Perhaps Mr. Rochester is standing at his window. Or walking in the orchard. Or in front of the house, I thought wildly. If I could only see him again!

I circled the orchard and grounds until I reached two stone **pillars**. From there I would be able to gaze

....

My path was now clear. I knew what I wanted to do.

an inn a hotel; a lodge

pillars columns

upon **majestic** Thornfield Hall. I crept over and peered around one of the pillars.

But I did not see a stately home. Thornfield was a blackened ruin!

The place was burned **beyond repair**. The lawns were flattened. The windows had no panes. The roof, chimney, and battlements had all crashed in. No wonder my letters had not been answered.

I wandered around the shattered walls. The damage must have happened months ago, allowing snow and rain inside. Grass and weeds now grew everywhere among the stones and rafters.

And where, oh, where, was the owner?

I returned to the nearby inn. Surely the innkeeper could give me some news.

"You know Thornfield Hall?" I asked him.

"Yes, ma'am," the middle-aged man replied.

"Is Mr. Rochester living there now?" I inquired. Of course I knew what the answer would be.

"Oh, no!" the innkeeper exclaimed. "No one is living there. It burned down last autumn." The man shook his head sadly. "I saw it happen myself."

....

majestic impressive, magnificent
beyond repair and it could not be fixed

"How did the fire start?" I asked.

The man edged closer to me. "Well, ma'am, perhaps you are aware that a lunatic lady was rumored to live in the house?" he asked quietly. "This lady, ma'am, turned out to be Mr. Edward Rochester's wife! That was discovered just as Mr. Rochester was about to marry the young governess living at Thornfield Hall."

"Did Mrs. Rochester have anything to do with the fire?" I demanded.

"It had to be her who set it," the man said. "The woman who took care of her was called Mrs. Poole. She was a trustworthy person, but **a heavy sleeper**. The mad lady was **cunning** and used to wait until Mrs. Poole was asleep. Then she would take the keys from Mrs. Poole's pocket, let herself out of her room, and go roaming about the house **doing mischief**.

"Last autumn, she made her way downstairs to the governess's chamber and set the bed on fire," the innkeeper continued. "Luckily, no one was sleeping in it. You see, the governess had run away two months before. Mr. Rochester had been very upset and tried to find her. But he never did.

---

a heavy sleeper she had a hard time waking up

cunning sneaky

doing mischief making trouble

"**He was a changed man** after the young lady fled, and wanted to be alone. He sent his housekeeper, Mrs. Fairfax, away to stay with friends and Miss Adèle, his ward, to school. **Then he shut himself up like a hermit** in Thornfield Hall." The innkeeper sighed heavily.

"Then he was at home when the fire broke out?" I asked.

"Yes, indeed. He got the servants out of their attic rooms safely, then went back to get his mad wife. She was standing on the roof, waving and shouting, with her long black hair **streaming** against the flames. Mr. Rochester climbed up to the roof and approached her. She yelled and jumped—and the next minute she lay smashed on the pavement below."

"Dead?" I whispered.

"Oh, yes! Dead as the stones on which her brains and blood were scattered." The man shuddered. "It was frightful! Mr. Rochester wouldn't leave the house until everyone was out. As he came down the staircase, there was a crash and everything fell. He was taken out alive, but one hand was crushed and his eyes were injured. It's

....

He was a changed man He did things differently
Then he shut himself up like a hermit He stayed alone
streaming moving

said he is now blind."

"Where does he live?" I asked urgently.

"At Ferndean, a manor house he owns. It's about thirty miles **off**. Old John and his wife, Mary, are the only servants there," the innkeeper told me.

I asked him to get a carriage ready for me at once. A carriage that would take me to Ferndean.

....

off away

Chapter Fourteen

I Go to Ferndean

Mr. Rochester had spoken to me in the past about Ferndean Manor. I arrived there just before dark. Cold rain was falling. As I had done at Thornfield, I left the coach a mile from Ferndean and walked the rest of the way.

I entered the grounds through iron gates and followed a grass-covered track in a forest of trees. **It stretched on and on.** Had I taken a wrong turn and lost my way?

But I kept walking and finally reached the **dank and decaying house**. The narrow front door opened. A figure came out into the twilight. He stretched his hand as if to feel whether it was raining. I recognized the man. It was Edward Rochester.

His hair was still dark, his posture still straight. But his face was desperate and brooding. He slowly walked

....

It stretched on and on. I walked for a long time.

dank and decaying wet and rotting

onto the grass, then groped his way back indoors.

I now drew near and knocked. John's wife opened the door.

"Mary," I said, "how are you?"

She looked as if she had seen a ghost. "Is it really you, Miss? Come at this late hour to this lonely place?" she asked.

I took her hand and followed her into the kitchen. There I told her and John what had happened to me since leaving Thornfield.

When the parlor bell rang, Mary filled a glass with water and put it on a tray with candles. "The master always has candles brought into the room at night, even though he is blind," she explained.

"Give me the tray," I said. "I will carry it in."

My heart beat wildly as I entered the gloomy parlor. Mr. Rochester's old dog, Pilot, pricked up his ears when I came in. He jumped up and almost knocked the tray from my hands.

I patted Pilot. "Lie down," I said quietly to the dog. Mr. Rochester turned **at the sound of the commotion**.

....

at the sound of the commotion when he heard the noise

"Give me the water, Mary," he said.

I handed him the glass. "Mary is in the kitchen," I said.

"Who is this?" he demanded. "Speak!"

"Pilot knows me, and John and Mary, too. I came this evening," I said.

Mr. Rochester grasped my hand. **"What madness has seized me?"** he cried. "Her fingers! Her small fingers!" He wrapped his arm around me. "Is it *Jane*? This is her shape, her size—"

"And this is her voice," I added. "She is all here— her heart, too! I am glad to be so near you again!"

"Jane Eyre! Jane Eyre!" he repeated. "My darling! It is a dream!"

I kissed him lovingly. "I have come back to you. And I am an independent woman now—quite rich."

He asked me many questions after supper: how I had been, how I had found him. But I gave him short **replies**. It was too late that night to **go into detail**.

Mary showed me to a guest room, where I slept well. The next morning, I joined Mr. Rochester for breakfast. Then we spent the morning outdoors.

....

What madness has seized me? Have I gone insane?
replies answers
go into detail tell him the entire story

Sitting in a sunny field, I described what had happened to me, from arriving at the Rivers' house to discovering my relatives. And he and I declared our love for each other again.

"Jane, will you marry me?" he asked.

"Yes!" I said.

He told me that he had begun to think I must have died. But a few days before, on Monday night, he prayed that he would find me somehow.

"**Your name burst from my lips**," he said. "As I said 'Jane!' three times, I heard your voice reply 'I am coming! Wait for me!' I felt as if **we had met in spirit**."

I did not tell him that I had heard his voice that same Monday night. The **coincidence** was too strange.

Reader, I married him. We had a quiet wedding with just a parson and a clerk. I wrote to Diana, Mary, and St. John Rivers to say what I had done. They understood my reasons and were happy for me.

Of course, I had not forgotten little Adèle. I visited her at school, and she was full of joy at seeing me. But

---

Your name burst from my lips I began to yell your name

we had met in spirit our souls were together, even though we were physically apart

coincidence connection

I found her thin and pale, and unhappy with the strict place. So I took her home with me and placed her in a kinder school. She made fine progress in her studies and came to visit us often.

My Edward and I were very happy together. I knew I had made the right decision in marrying him.

After two years of marriage, the sight in one of Mr. Rochester's eyes began to clear slightly. Under a doctor's care, he finally **regained some sight in that eye**. It was not enough to read or write much, but he **could make his way around on his own**.

And later, when our baby boy was put in his arms, Mr. Rochester was able to see his first-born child!

....

regained some sight in that eye was able to see better

could make his way around on his own was able to walk through the house by himself

BEFORE YOU MOVE ON...

1. **Inference** Jane leaves her cousins to find Mr. Rochester. What does this show about what Jane values most?

2. **Author's Style** Reread page 114. How does the author show that Jane and Mr. Rochester have a deep love?

2006 Series
Toby Stephenson
6 episodes